I'm
scared!

Also by Bel Mooney

I don't want to!
I can't find it!
It's not fair!
But you promised!
Why not?
I know!
I wish!

for older readers

The Voices of Silence

BEL MOONEY

I'm scared!

Illustrated by Margaret Chamberlain

MAMMOTH

For Tom Woodward

First published in Great Britain 1994
by Methuen Children's Books Ltd
Published 1995 by Mammoth
an imprint of Reed International Books Ltd
Michelin House, 81 Fulham Road, London SW3 6RB
and Auckland, Melbourne, Singapore and Toronto

Reprinted 1995 (three times), 1996 (four times), 1997

ISBN 0 7497 2330 0

A CIP catalogue record for this title
is available from the British Library

Printed and bound in Great Britain
by Cox & Wyman Ltd, Reading, Berkshire

Contents

I'm scared!

. . . of the dark

'I'm not scared of anything – not me!' said Kitty, folding her arms, and standing by the back door.

Outside the wind was moaning, and rain rattled on the kitchen window.

'Yes, you are,' said Daniel.

'No, I'm not,' said Kitty.

'Kitty thinks she's big and brave!' jeered her brother.

'I *know* I am,' shouted Kitty.

'Go out into the garden then!' said Daniel, with a big grin. 'Walk to the end of the garden and back, on your own!'

Kitty looked outside. It was dark. The only light in the garden came from the kitchen window – all strange and yellowish in the rain.

Wooooo-woooo went the wind.

'It's only our old garden,' said Kitty. 'Who's afraid of that? It's not worth doing!'

'*Dark* out there!' teased Daniel.

Kitty gulped.

'I dare you,' said Daniel.

'No – I don't want to', said Kitty.

'Kitty's scared! Scaredy-Kitty-Kat!' Daniel laughed and laughed.

Kitty couldn't bear it.

'I jolly well will – so there!' she yelled, and pulled open the back door. She had taken one step away from the door, when she heard Daniel turn the key in the lock. And to be really mean, he pulled down the blind at the window, so there was much less light streaming out.

It was dark. And cold. And rainy. And still

the wind went on sighing – as if it was sad.

Without stopping to think, Kitty began to walk. The garden seemed very different in this strange half-light. The bushes looked big and black, like huge animals waiting to pounce. The wind made them rustle . . .

What was that? A lion? A tiger?

Kitty knew it was only the redcurrant bush and the flowering shrubs – but her heart began to thud, and she started to walk more quickly.

What was that? A dinosaur?

Kitty knew it was only the wheelbarrow, upside down with a few plastic plant-pots dumped higgledy-piggledy on it – but her mouth went dry, and she turned her walk into a skip.

The sky had a few streaks of light in it – pink and yellow – and the trees stood out very blackly. They seemed to wave their bare arms in the air, as if to say, 'Go back!'

Kitty remembered all those lovely illustrations in children's books, where the old trees in the forest wore scary faces, and their roots and branches were like arms and legs, waiting to reach out . . .

She wished she hadn't thought of them. She didn't want to remember them. Because it was easy to look at these trees – the friendly trees they liked to climb in their own garden – and know for sure that they had faces too.

And the faces weren't friendly. Not at all.

There was a small creaking noise as the swing Dad had made blew backwards and forwards, backwards and forwards – as if some invisible person was pushing it . . .

Kitty took a deep breath, and started to run. In the daytime their garden seemed quite small, really – just an ordinary garden with a hedge all around, bordering on to the neighbours' gardens. But now in the dark it seemed enormous, with vast shadowy corners in which anything could hide.

What made it worse was that William's house was in total darkness. She knew they had all gone to stay with his aunt and uncle, and wouldn't be back until tomorrow. So – there was no help there.

But help for what?

Kitty ran as fast as her little legs would carry her. At the end of the garden was the shed.

It was a nice garden shed, with a door in the middle and a window each side, like a little house.

She loved the way Mum and Dad hung the gardening tools neatly on the wall inside, and there was a bench with all sorts of interesting things on it – like balls of string and hammers and nails and tiny flower pots. It was a good place to play. In the day.

But now it wasn't like a friendly little house. It could be a dark hut . . . in a scary story . . . lived in by a wicked witch . . . .

Kitty stopped before she reached it. She was panting now, and very chilly, with rain runniing down her face. 'I'm *scared*,' she whispered. 'I'm scared of the d-d-dark.' She wanted to cry.

Then she turned to run back to the house – and something surprising happened. Mum and Dad must have been in different rooms, because suddenly all the lights went on at once. Their home glowed, like a beacon.

As the blaze of light hit the garden, lighting up all the things Kitty had passed, she saw exactly what they were. The redcurrant bush. The flowering shrubs. The upside-down wheelbarrow. The nice old trees, one of them with the swing hanging from it.

The wind still sighed, and the bushes still rustled, but now they seemed to be friendly, telling Kitty that she should be inside.

Wooohooooo . . . gooooo hooooooome!

Home! With the bright lights, and the fire, and sausages and mash for supper, and Mum and Dad, and Mr Tubs the bear waiting upstairs.

Kitty ran forward – only this time she wasn't scared. Not a bit. She knew she had been silly, and she wanted her supper.

Funnily, it only took a minute or so to reach the back door. When she tried the handle, it was unlocked. She pushed open the door and went inside.

'KITTY!' cried Mum, looking at her wet jumper and hair.

'Where've you been?' asked Dad, 'I can't

believe you were so silly as to go out without a coat.'

'And in the dark!' said Mum.

Kitty sat down, looking very calm. 'I wasn't scared,' she said.

Then she saw Daniel looking at her. He thought she was going to tell on him. He knew he'd get into trouble, because Dad couldn't stand silly dares. He was *scared*.

'Dan thought he'd dropped his pen,' said Kitty, 'and I went to look for it – because he was scared to go out.'

Her brother opened his mouth like a fish, then closed it again. Kitty knew he wouldn't dare to tell the truth!

I'm scared!

. . . of the people

It was just two weeks before Christmas, and all the classrooms were decorated with cotton wool snow, cut-outs of candles and kings and angels, and little silver trees. It was very exciting.

But the most exciting thing of all was also the most frightening. The School Play. The children had been learning and rehearsing for weeks, and now this was the big moment.

'I bet I forget my words!' said Rosie.

'I think I'll fall over when I have to walk across the stage,' said Anita.

'I know I'm going to giggle!' said Kitty.

They all laughed, but William looked very miserable. 'I'm scared,' he said in a small voice.

'What of?' asked Rosie, in a big voice, which said: 'don't-be-such-a-baby'.

William shook his head. Kitty felt sorry for him, and she knew she had to be on his side. Because even though Rosie and Anita were her best friends, William lived next door and was the friend she'd had for longest.

So she said, 'He's scared of all the people, of course! And we all are.'

'I'm not,' said Rosie.

William walked away.

The trouble was, William had one of the biggest parts. He had to play Joseph. In this Nativity play Joseph was given lots of words, and had to be very fat and jolly. William was a good actor, with a big voice – until he got nervous.

Rosie was one of the Three Kings and didn't have too much to say. But she had a splendid costume, and held her golden casket high.

Anita was an angel, even though she had a different religion. Her family gave presents at Diwali, not Christmas. But the headmistress said that there were good spirits in all religions, and so Anita was very happy to dress in white and stand there looking pretty, and sing.

Kitty had to play a . . . (oh dear, it made Dan and Mum and Dad laugh so much!) . . . a donkey.

She had to get into this stupid scratchy donkey suit and sit there in the 'stable', looking at the doll which played the baby Jesus. And that's all.

So she wasn't scared a bit.

After school they all ate sandwiches, and then everybody started to get ready. The teachers were rushing around, making sure everything was ready. Some older children were helping with the scenery. It was all very busy and exciting.

But Kitty saw that William's face was white. 'Come and talk to me,' she whispered.

They walked along the corridor, and William bit his lip.

'There'll be so many people,' he said, 'and as soon as I think of them all – all those faces watching me – I forget what I have to say.'

'Don't think of them!' said Kitty.

'I can't help it,' said William miserably. 'They are all *there*, in front of me, and there's nothing to stop me seeing them.'

'Cheer up,' said Kitty. 'You're supposed to be a jolly Joseph!'

'How can I be jolly when I'm scared?' muttered William.

There was a buzz in the hall, as the mothers and fathers took their places. All the children waited at the sides of the stage. They were so excited they wanted to burst. It felt so Christmassy too – the sound of carols from the piano, making all of them remember all the Christmasses they had known.

Even though she was hot inside her donkey suit, Kitty felt very happy. She knew that Mum and Dad were out there, sitting with William's Mum and Dad, waiting to feel proud.

'I feel sick,' whispered William in her ear.

'Don't be silly,' said Kitty. But she felt worried.

Soon the curtain was up, and the Nativity

play had begun. Kitty heard the innkeeper tell Mary and Joseph there was no room at the inn, and William had to protest, which he did. But she knew his voice was a bit wavery. He was very scared. Then the innkeeper's wife went running out, and told them they could sleep in the stable.

That was the point at which the inside curtain went up, to show Kitty sitting on a little heap of straw, next to a large toy sheep. A little chuckle went through the audience. 'Huh,' thought Kitty, 'it would be me who's made to look an idiot!'

The play went on. Then came the moment when Joseph had to make a speech about the cold weather, and how the sky above was full of stars, like jewels in the sky. Then he was supposed to make a little joke and say that the stars were Mary's jewels, and the animals her fine servants.

Through the mouth of her donkey suit Kitty could see his face, looking funny with the false beard. He was staring at all the people like a frightened rabbit. Even before it happened she knew he was going to forget something. His mouth opened and closed. He couldn't remember. There was a horrible moment of silence.

Kitty had to do something . . .

21

'*Ee-ore*,' said Kitty.

William looked at her in amazement. So did the girl who played Mary. Kitty put up one 'hoof' to her nose and pretended to scratch. 'EE-ORE' she brayed, more loudly.

The audience started to laugh. They thought this was part of the play. And Mary and Joseph laughed too.

Looking at the funny donkey, William remembered his words. ' . . . *and, my dear wife, these faithful animals are your fine servants – so we aren't really poor at all*,' he said, in a good, loud voice.

From that moment on he was better. Kitty stared at him, and every time he saw her

peering through her donkey mouth he looked very merry, waiting for her to bray again.

But she didn't need to. He forgot the people, and remembered all his words.

At the end, when all the children lined up on stage for their bow, the audience clapped and cheered. Kitty felt very proud when she saw Mum and Dad beaming from the second row.

When they were taking their costumes off, the headmistress came to say how pleased she

was. But when she got to Kitty she gave a tiny little frown, and said, 'I wasn't too sure about your interruptions, Kitty, although I suppose it didn't do any harm.'

Thank goodness William was listening, and he spoke up just as loudly as if he was still on stage.

'That was to help me, Miss Jones,' he said, 'Kitty knows that if you laugh, you can't be scared!'

I'm scared!

. . . of the monster

He was definitely there – Kitty knew it. One night he just popped into her dream, and when she woke up she knew he was under the bed! '*Muu-uuuum!*' she called.

Mum came in, in her dressing gown, looking sleepy. 'What's the matter, my love? Did you have a bad dream?' she whispered.

'I dreamed I was being chased by a monster,' said Kitty, 'and then when I ran into my room, he followed me. And . . . and . . . oh, Mum . . .'

'What is it?' asked Mum, in a soft voice.

'He's still under the bed!' hissed Kitty.

Mum smiled. 'Well, we'll just have a look, shall we?' She went down on her hands and knees and looked under the bed. She pulled out . . . one sock, two slippers, a little plastic knight from Kitty's castle, a pencil, a bouncy ball – and Mr Tubs.

'I know what happened. You had your dream, you tossed and turned, Mr Tubs fell out, and because he's just a good bear, he rolled under the bed to find all these other things you'd lost! There wasn't a monster under the bed. There was only Mr Tubs!'

'Oh,' Kitty said.

'Go back to sleep now, there's a good girl,' said Mum. And she went back to bed too.

Kitty hugged Mr Tubs tightly. 'I know what you were doing,' she whispered in his ear, 'you were making sure the Monster didn't come out and get me. Weren't you?'

But Mr Tubs didn't say a word, and quite soon Kitty went off to sleep again.

In the morning, when her alarm clock went *ping*, she lay for a few moments thinking about the Monster. She didn't want to put her legs out of the bed. Just in case.

At last Mum came to the bedroom door. 'Hurry up, Kit – you'll be late for school,' she called.

'Mum! Please come here,' said Kitty.

'Oh, what IS it?'

'Mum, I'm scared of the Monster,' said Kitty.

'Oh, don't be so SILLY!' said Mum. And she rushed across, threw back the bedclothes, and quickly pulled Kitty out of bed.

'I thought we sorted that out last night,' she

said with a sigh. 'Now just hurry up!'

Kitty didn't think about the Monster all day in school, but when she got home she decided she wouldn't go to her room, she would stay downstairs.

Dad was reading the newspaper in the sitting room. Kitty crept up and told him everything. He didn't laugh.

'Go and get your drawing book,' he said.

When Kitty came back he said, 'Now, I want you to draw me a picture of this monster.'

Kitty bit her pencil and thought. 'I can't,' she said.

'Why?' asked Dad.

'Because . . . well, you know he's not really real, Dad. He's in my head.'

'But he's under the bed as well?'

'Yes,' said Kitty firmly.

'Well then, you CAN draw a picture of him for me. Go on!' said Dad. 'I want to meet this old chap.'

Kitty thought for a moment then started to draw. A funny fat body . . . a round face with two sharp teeth . . . big round eyes . . . pointed ears . . . a tail with a spiky thing on the end.

Dad smiled. 'Well, he looks rather jolly to me. What colour is he?'

'Green,' said Kitty.

'He would be, of course,' said Dad. 'A bit like a dragon.'

Kitty looked at her drawing, and smiled. 'He looks funny,' she said. And he did – a tubby creature with a smiley mouth, despite those teeth. A nice Magic Monster.

'What does he like to eat?' asked Dad.

'Er . . . baked beans!' said Kitty.

'Good taste,' said Dad. 'So why don't you put some out for him tonight? Just to keep him happy!'

'Our secret?' whispered Kitty. Dad nodded.

Kitty couldn't wait to get to bed. After Mum had read her a story, and said goodnight, Dad came in carrying something behind his back. It was a dish of cold baked beans, with a spoon in it. He put it on the floor by Kitty's bed, knelt down, bent his head, and spoke to the Monster.

'OK, old chum. We know you're nice and friendly really, and nobody's ever discovered it before. So we've brought you a midnight feast. Mind you, don't wake Kitty up, will you?'

Then he looked up at Kitty. 'He's really sweet – and he's very pleased!' said Dad, leaning forward to give her a big kiss.

'Now . . . sleep time, Kitty-Kat.'

Kitty snuggled down with Mr Tubs. She thought about the Monster, but all she could see was the funny creature she had drawn, and *he* was so friendly she couldn't possibly be scared any more. So she went to sleep.

Early, before her alarm went off, she woke. Quickly she swung her legs round, and bent to look at the baked beans. They were still in the dish.

Kitty loved cold beans – and it took her two

minutes to eat the lot. Then she got back into bed, and pretended to be asleep.

Dad tiptoed in, and gave her a little shake. 'Wake up, pet! Guess what? The beans have gone!'

Kitty sat up, trying to look innocent. There was tomato sauce all round her mouth. 'Have they? Well, that just proves there's a Monster!' she said.

Dad grinned. 'Oh, I never doubted it,' he said, 'because little Monsters come in all shapes and sizes, and they're usually lovely when you get to know them! Aren't they, Kitty?'

And of course, she had to agree.

I'm scared!

. . . of the teacher

They had a new form teacher, called Miss Robinson, and Kitty didn't like that at all. Mrs Smith was expecting a baby, and had left. Kitty really loved Mrs Smith. So she decided the new teacher was going to be horrible.

'And I'll be horrible too,' said Kitty.

Miss Robinson was very young, and had a very stiff, cross way of walking and talking. Kitty hated that.

On her very first day, she asked who would like to do jobs in the classroom. Everybody put up a hand, except Kitty. Miss Robinson noticed.

'What's your name?' she asked. Kitty didn't speak. Rosie called out, 'That's Kitty, Miss.'

'Well, Kitty, why haven't you got your hand up?'

Kitty shrugged, folded her arms, and said, 'I don't want to.'

'Oh, I see,' said the teacher – and frowned.

That day Kitty was naughty. She talked even when she was told not to. She passed a note to Rosie. She pretended not to have a pen, when all the time it was in her pencil case.

The next day was just the same . . . and the next. Kitty knew that you can be naughty even without doing much – just by looking cross and sulky and bored in class.

And so she went on – all week. The other children began to copy, too.

When Miss Robinson asked her why she was

looking out of the window, Kitty said, 'Dunno.'

When Miss Robinson wondered why Kitty didn't have her own rubber, Kitty said, 'I can't find it.'

When Miss Robinson said Kitty must not stand on the desk at playtime, Kitty said, 'Why not?'

When Miss Robinson told Kitty she was being very cheeky, Kitty said, 'I know!'

When Miss Robinson got very cross and told Kitty she would have to miss games, so she could finish her sums, Kitty yelled, 'It's not fair!'

It was Friday now, and at last Miss Robinson lost her temper with Kitty. All the children went very, very quiet, as the teacher shouted. She told Kitty she was the naughtiest little girl she had ever met, a show-off too. She said she didn't deserve to go to such a nice school. She said . . . oh, so many bad things!

And Kitty felt smaller and smaller. All the children were looking at her. It was awful . . . and deep down she wanted to cry.

Actually, Miss Robinson looked as if she wanted to cry too – or was it just that she was red with anger?

After school Kitty was very quiet and Mum asked what was wrong. Kitty told her that she'd had a bad week. When Mum asked why, Kitty said the teacher had been horrible to her, *really* horrible.

I'm not going to school on Monday,' she said, starting to cry, 'because I'm really scared of her now!'

'Not you, Kitty!' said Mum, 'You always say you aren't afraid of anything!'

But it was true. Every time Kitty thought of the way Miss Robinson had told her off, she had a bad feeling in her tummy.

As usual on Saturday morning they went to the shops. The High Street was crowded. Kitty stayed very close to Mum. Suddenly, though, she pulled Mum's sleeve. 'There's Mrs Smith,' she said. 'Can I go and talk to her?'

'Yes – she's right by the butcher's and I have to go in there,' said Mum.

Kitty's Mum said hallo to Mrs Smith, then went to join the queue. Kitty felt quite shy at seeing her old teacher – her tummy was so big now!

'And how are you, Kitty? How's school?' asked Mrs Smith.

'All right,' said Kitty.

'What about your new teacher?'

Kitty frowned, looked down and shook her head.

'I'm scared of her!' Kitty blurted out. Then she told Mrs Smith everything that had happened. Everything.

'So you were a naughty girl?'

Kitty nodded. 'I didn't want *her*. I wanted *you* to come back,' she said, in a tiny voice.

'But Kitty – I'm going to have my baby, and stay at home for a while. I can't come back. You know that, don't you?'

Kitty nodded.

'So are you going to go on being scared of Miss Robinson?'

Kitty nodded.

'But Kitty, you know the truth? It's not you who's afraid of Miss Robinson, it's Miss Robinson who's afraid of *you*!'

Kitty looked up, amazed. Mrs Smith was smiling her lovely warm smile.

'Teachers don't get scared,' said Kitty.

'Oh yes, they do,' said Mrs Smith, 'especially when they're young and new. So will you do something for me? Will you *promise* you'll look after Miss Robinson – just for me?'

Of course, Kitty had to say yes. All weekend she thought of what Mrs Smith had said, and imagined Miss Robinson at home, feeling scared of Monday.

So, by the time Monday came, Kitty knew just what she had to do. She was friendly, she put her hand up quickly, she was neat, she was nice. And all the other children followed her lead.

Of course, Miss Robinson soon stopped frowning. Then Kitty decided her smile was just as nice as Mrs Smith's.

I'm scared!

. . . they'll get me

Kitty's friend, Anita Attra, was quiet and shy – not at all like Kitty or Rosie. Even though Kitty was little, while Rosie was tall and quite tough, they both felt they had to look after Anita.

They loved going to Anita's house to play. Kitty liked the wonderful smell of spices in the kitchen, which always made her hungry. So Mrs Attra gave them lovely round sticky sweets, and sometimes they had poppadums too. Kitty loved poppadums, and the special nan bread they could dip into Mrs Attra's tasty sauces.

Rosie said what she liked best was the fact that Anita didn't have lots of noisy brothers and a fashionable big sister, like she did!

'I can't get a bit of peace,' she said.

One day Kitty noticed that Anita was even more quiet than usual.

'What's wrong?' she asked.

Anita just shook her head.

But after school, she rushed off without saying goodbye, which was very strange. Mrs Attra used to meet her, but in the last couple of weeks all Anita's three little brothers had been ill with a tummy bug, so Anita went home by herself. It was a very short way. She had to cross with the lollipop man, walk along the road, turn right by the supermarket, walk a bit further, and then she was home.

She told Kitty and Rose she felt very grown-up.

The next day she seemed very unhappy, and the next, and the next. She hardly spoke to anybody. Kitty thought her eyes looked red, but when she asked what was the matter Anita just muttered she was getting a cold.

'A cold? In September?' Kitty thought.

At last Rosie couldn't bear it any more. 'Come on, Kit – we've got to find out what's wrong.' she said.

So at dinner time they marched up to Anita and said she had to tell them what was bothering her.

At first she shook her head. At last, she burst into tears.

'I'm . . . I'm . . . scared,' she cried.

'What of?' asked Kitty.

'I'm scared . . . they'll *get* me,' Anita sniffed.

'Who?' asked Rosie.

'Those girls,' said Anita, 'and one boy, too.'

She told them what had happened. Each

night three girls and one boy – all of them big, about *fourteen* she said – waited for her round the corner, and said horrible things to her.

'They said they're going to get me,' whispered Anita.

'Why didn't you tell us?' asked Kitty.

'They warned me not to.'

'Oh, they did, did they?' said Rosie, folding her arms.

'Big bullies!' said Kitty.

She felt very angry, and knew something had to be done. When Anita went running in at the bell, Kitty stopped to whisper to Rosie. Then Rosie started to smile all over her face and rushed off to use the school payphone.

That afternoon, Kitty passed lots of notes, but she was so careful, Miss Robinson didn't see. Tom, the tallest boy in the class (who used to call her Shrimp) looked at her and nodded. So did Susie, who was so brilliant at netball. And William, too.

Kitty even got a message to her brother Daniel, who walked home from school with her now, because Mum was at work.

After school they all walked out of the gates with Anita. She was just turning to say goodbye when she stopped, amazed. There by the gate were Rosie's sister, and her three brothers, all with big grins on their faces.

'Hi – Sara . . . Robbie . . . Ben . . . Sam!' said Rosie.

Sara was thirteen, and wore wonderful leggings and trainers. Robbie was fourteen, Ben was sixteen, and they were both brilliant footballers. Kitty liked them all. But Sam was her favourite. He was eighteen, and very good-looking. He wore his hair in long dreadlocks, and played guitar in a band.

'I rounded them all up like you said,

Rosy-Posy,' said Sam, 'so now we can take Anita home!'

Anita looked at the four of them, then round at Rosie, Kitty, Daniel, Tom, Susie and William.

'But . . .' she began.

'No buts,' said Kitty.

They all set off. The lollipop man stared, and so did the other children. Nobody knew what was going on. But Kitty felt like a general at the head of an army. She walked ahead with Anita, and when they got to the corner she made a signal to Rosie.

The others hid, while she and Anita went on alone. The four bullies were waiting by the shop. They looked so *big*. And they had horrid looks on their faces.

'Here she comes,' said the first girl.

'She's got somebody with her,' jeered the second girl.

'I thought we warned you!' said the third girl.

The boy stepped forward and started to say bad words. Kitty wasn't scared. She stood in front of Anita, and said, 'This is my idea, not hers. I thought you ought to know she's got lots and lots of friends, and they all want to meet you!'

She whistled and everybody stepped out from behind the corner. The bullies backed away.

'Are you scared?' shouted Kitty.

''Course they are,' said big Sam, in a quiet voice. 'Bullies are only brave when they think they're safe.'

'Well, you will be safe,' said Kitty, pointing at the nearest big girl, 'as long as you keep away from our Anita!'

And from then on, of course, they did.

I'm scared!

. . . of ghosts

Kitty was in a bad mood again, because Mum had just told her that Melissa was coming to stay.

'*For two whole days and nights*!' groaned Kitty.

Melissa was Kitty's cousin, and Kitty didn't like her one bit. She was always good, and kept her pretty clothes clean, and didn't like playing wild games in the garden, like Kitty.

'Can we come and play with you, William?' asked Kitty.

'Um . . . but Melissa's really boring,' said William.

'Oh, please,' said Kitty.

'Melissa won't play make-up games, or anything,' William protested.

'I know,' said Kitty, gloomily.

Melissa arrived with a big suitcase.

'How long are you staying?' asked Kitty.

'I like to change my clothes,' said Melissa.

'I know,' said Kitty, gloomily.

In fact, what got her most annoyed about Melissa was that Melissa always *knew* everything. Ages ago she said there was no such thing as the tooth fairy, or Father Christmas, or angels, or anything like that.

'But you can't be sure,' said Kitty, who

secretly liked to believe in everything. 'Why not?'

'It's just babyish,' said Melissa.

Dad and Mum took them out for tea to a beautiful little village quite near the town. There was a very old church there, with a churchyard full of pretty trees and old gravestones. Whenever they went there, Kitty liked to wander in the graveyard with Mum and Dad. It was a peaceful place. She liked to make up stories about all the people who had lived there.

But Melissa hung back. 'Ugh, I don't want to go in there,' she said.

'Why?' asked Kitty. 'Go on – why?'

'I'm scared,' whispered Melissa.

'Scared? What of?' Kitty laughed.

'The ghosts!' said Melissa.

'Well, *that's* babyish,' said Kitty.

Dad was listening. 'Oh, Melissa love, there's no such thing as ghosts,' he said.

'Anyway,' said Mum, 'this is such a pretty place, any ghosts would have to be nice, friendly ones!'

'You shouldn't make jokes like that,' said Melissa, with her nose in the air.

'If I was a ghost I'd be scared of *you*, Melissa,' said Kitty.

'Very funny,' said Melissa.

When they got home, Melissa said she was going upstairs to change her clothes.

'What!' said Kitty. 'I thought we might play in the garden with William.'

'I don't want to!' said Melissa.

She came down ten minutes later wearing a beautiful pure white cotton dress, with pink embroidery on the collar. Kitty still had on her shorts and tee-shirt.

'*Oooo* Melissa – you look like a ghost,' she said.

It was then that Kitty had her naughty idea. Putting Melissa in front of the television, she ran upstairs and set to work. It didn't take her very long, and soon she was able to close the spare-room door very quietly.

When at last it was time to go to bed, Kitty asked Mum if they could take up apples and some juice for a feast in her room.

'I thought I'd tell Melissa a story before she goes to bed,' said Kitty.

'There's a good girl,' said Mum, pleased Kitty was being nice to her cousin.

They carried up the tray, and sat down on Kitty's bed.

'What story?' said Melissa, munching her apple.

'It's a ghost story,' whispered Kitty, 'a *true* ghost story: about this house, Melissa.'

Melissa's eyes opened wide.

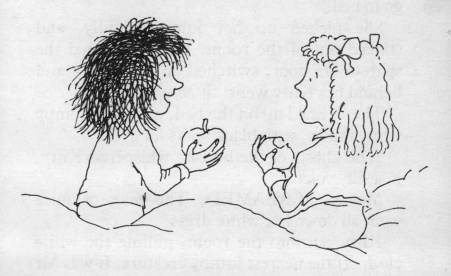

'Once upon a time,' Kitty began, 'there was a family of four . . . er . . . little creatures . . .'

'What creatures?' asked Melissa.

'Never mind! Just listen! Anyway, they all lived in this house for years and years, and then something *terrible* happened – something so terrible and frightening I can't even tell you about it – and the four creatures turned into ghosts, and ever since then they've been here . . .'

'Where?' asked Melissa.

'In the spare room' whispered Kitty, 'Where *you* are sleeping, Melissa.'

Melissa jumped up. 'You're just being silly,' she shouted, 'and I don't like it. I'm going to go to bed!'

She picked up her juice carefully, and stalked out of the room. Melissa opened the spare-room door, switched on the light – and behind her Kitty went: '*Woooooooh!*'

There, lined up on the bed, were four lumpy white things, with black spots for eyes.

'The ghosts of the house,' whispered Kitty, in a silly voice.

Melissa SCREAMED. The mug of juice went all down her white dress.

Kitty ran into the room, pulling the white cloth off the nearest lumpy creature. It was Mr

Tubs. She had dressed him and three other cuddly toys as ghosts!

'You see, Melissa – I told you ghosts were friendly!' she grinned. 'There's no need to be scared at all!'

I'm scared!

. . . no one will like me

'I hate Daniel,' shouted Kitty, stamping her foot.

'That's a naughty thing to say,' said Mum. 'You don't hate your brother.'

'I do! He's mean to me,' said Kitty. Then she went up to her room to sulk.

The truth was, Daniel had been being a bit horrid lately.

There were lots of little ways . . . for

example, he *told* on Kitty, because he caught her taking the last chocolate mousse from the fridge. Then she got into trouble, and he grinned. They argued, and Dad said, 'Be quiet, Kitty!' even though Daniel was making as much noise! Dan grinned again, which made Kitty crosser than ever.

A bit later she decided she would try to make friends, because she wanted him to play cards. She even said 'please'. But Dan shook his head and said her games were boring.

The last straw was when Mum said neither of them could watch television, because Daniel had to do some homework.

'It's not fair!' yelled Kitty.

Daniel made a face at her when Mum's back was turned.

That's when Kitty decided she really did hate her brother.

So now Kitty cuddled Mr Tubs, and mumbled bad things about Dan into his lovely soft fur. 'I wish you were real, because then you could bite him!' she whispered.

Mr Tubs seemed to frown.

'He's been getting all Mum and Dad's attention,' Kitty went on, feeling unhappy. 'Just because he's going to this silly old new school tomorrow. I hope its horrible!'

Mr Tubs seemed to growl.

'He thinks he's so grown-up!' mumbled Kitty.

Mr Tubs didn't say anything, because his fur was getting wet with Kitty's tears.

A bit later she decided to go downstairs. So she tucked Mr Tubs under her arm and tiptoed along the landing.

Daniel's door was open. Kitty stopped. Her brother was standing quite still by his chair, staring down at the new uniform for big school, which Mum had laid out, after sewing on the name tapes.

He stared and stared, with a funny look on his face.

Then he heard a floorboard creak, and looked up, and saw Kitty. He went pink.

It was very strange.

'Go away,' he said.

'Why?' she asked, stepping into the room.

'Because I'm busy,' he said.

'But you're just staring at your new uniform,' she said.

Then Daniel's face went bright red. 'No, I'm not,' he mumbled.

It was then that Kitty began to guess what was going on. 'Don't you want to go to the school?' she asked.

She knew that Mum and Dad had chosen this school because they thought it was better

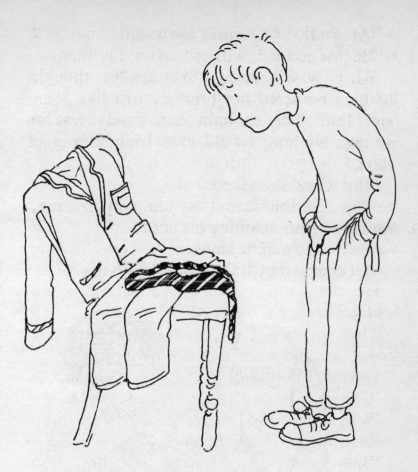

than the other one he could have gone to. But he would not be going with his friends. Mum told him that he would make new friends, so it didn't matter.

Dan flopped down on his bed. His face was so red, Kitty thought he might burst. And his eyes looked very bright.

'Are you . . . *worried*?' she asked.

He just nodded, without saying anything.

Kitty was amazed. She always thought nothing bothered her brother. Just like Mum and Dad. She thought her family was so strong. Nothing would ever frighten any of *them*.

'But why?' she asked.

'I'm . . . I'm scared no one will like me,' muttered Dan, hanging his head.

He looked as if he might cry.

'Of course they'll like you!' said Kitty.

'I'm scared they won't' said Dan. 'And I won't make any friends, and the teachers will be strict, and everything!'

Now the old bad Kitty wanted to dance around the room, laughing and chanting, 'Daniel's scared! Daniel's scared! Scaredy-Danny, Daredy-Scanny!'

But the new Kitty, who was growing up herself, wanted to make him feel better, even though he had been so horrible. She knew now he'd only been so mean because he was worried. That's all.

So first she shoved Mr Tubs at him, and said, 'Look after him for a bit. You remember when you borrowed him because you had a cold? He made you feel better.' Dan nodded, and just took the bear. (You see, he knew nobody is *ever* too old to cuddle a toy!)

Then Kitty ran downstairs and burst into the kitchen, where she had a long talk with Mum, and gave her special, secret instructions. After that she rushed into her bedroom, and closed the door.

When at last it was time for supper, Kitty went to Daniel's room to tell him. He was sitting on his bed with Mr Tubs beside him, sorting out his pencil case. He looked a bit happier. Kitty knew it was because of Mr Tubs.

They opened the kitchen door, and Daniel looked amazed. Mum had set the table nicely, with a proper cloth, and the best china – and there was a candle burning in the middle.

'It's a party!' crowed Kitty.

'Why?' asked Dan.

'To celebrate you going to your new school!' she said.

At Daniel's place was an enormous good luck card she had made him. It had a funny picture of Dan riding along on the back of an enormous black cat, into the new school gates. And there were smiley faces all round.

Daniel beamed. But when Mum and Dad were both busy at the cooker, serving the special chicken meal, he leaned across and whispered, 'Thanks Kit – but don't ever tell anyone I felt scared, will you? Promise!'

'Hah! IF you promise you'll be nice to me!' said the old bad Kitty.

A Selected List of Fiction from Mammoth

While every effort is made to keep prices low, it is sometimes necessary to increase prices at short notice. Mandarin Paperbacks reserves the right to show new retail prices on covers which may differ from those previously advertised in the text or elsewhere.

The prices shown below were correct at the time of going to press.

☐ 7497 1421 2	**Betsey Biggalow is Here!**	Malorie Blackman	£2.99
☐ 7497 0366 0	**Dilly the Dinosaur**	Tony Bradman	£2.99
☐ 7497 0137 4	**Flat Stanley**	Jeff Brown	£2.99
☐ 7497 0983 9	**The Real Tilly Beany**	Annie Dalton	£2.99
☐ 7497 0592 2	**The Peacock Garden**	Anita Desai	£2.99
☐ 7497 0054 8	**My Naughty Little Sister**	Dorothy Edwards	£2.99
☐ 7497 0723 2	**The Little Prince (colour ed.)**	A. Saint-Exupery	£3.99
☐ 7497 0305 9	**Bill's New Frock**	Anne Fine	£2.99
☐ 7497 1718 1	**My Grandmother's Stories**	Adèle Geras	£2.99
☐ 7497 2395 5	**Flow**	Pippa Goodheart	£2.99
☐ 7497 0041 6	**The Quiet Pirate**	Andrew Matthews	£2.99
☐ 7497 1930 3	**The Jessame Stories**	Julia Jarman	£2.99
☐ 7497 0420 9	**I Don't Want To!**	Bel Mooney	£2.99
☐ 7497 1496 4	**Miss Bianca in the Orient**	Margery Sharp	£2.99
☐ 7497 0048 3	**Friends and Brothers**	Dick King Smith	£2.99
☐ 7497 0795 X	**Owl Who Was Afraid of the Dark**	Jill Tomlinson	£2.99

All these books are available at your bookshop or newsagent, or can be ordered direct from the address below. Just tick the titles you want and fill in the form below.

Cash Sales Department, PO Box 5, Rushden, Northants NN10 6YX.
Fax: 01933 414047   :   Phone: 01933 414000.

Please send cheque, payable to 'Reed Book Services Ltd.', or postal order for purchase price quoted and allow the following for postage and packing:

£1.00 for the first book, 50p for the second; **FREE POSTAGE AND PACKING FOR THREE BOOKS OR MORE PER ORDER.**

NAME (Block letters) ....

ADDRESS ....

....

☐ I enclose my remittance for ....

☐ I wish to pay by Access/Visa Card Number

Expiry Date

Signature ....
Please quote our reference: MAND